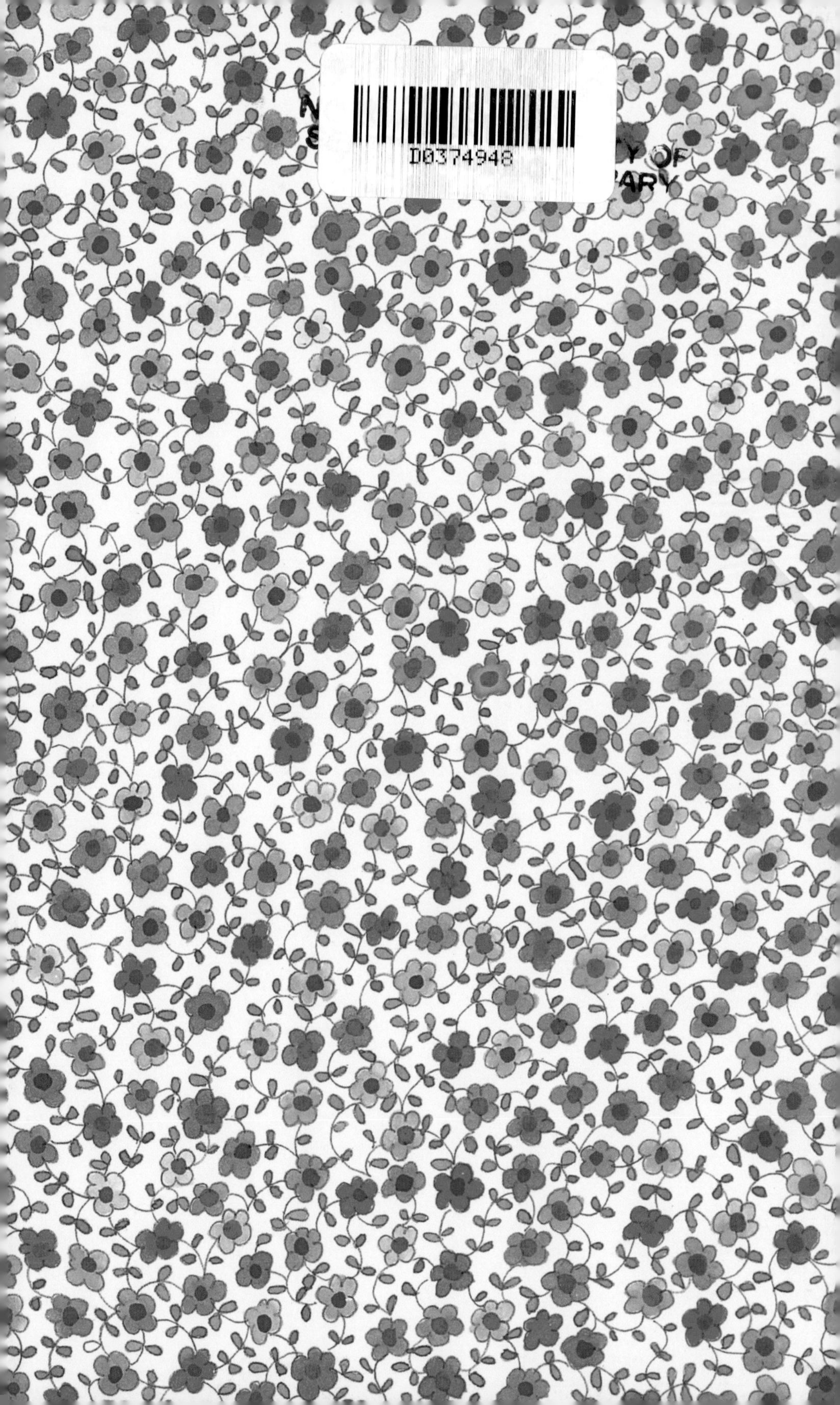
D0374948

Ruby Red Shoes

A Very Aware Hare

KATE KNAPP

Doubleday Books for Young Readers

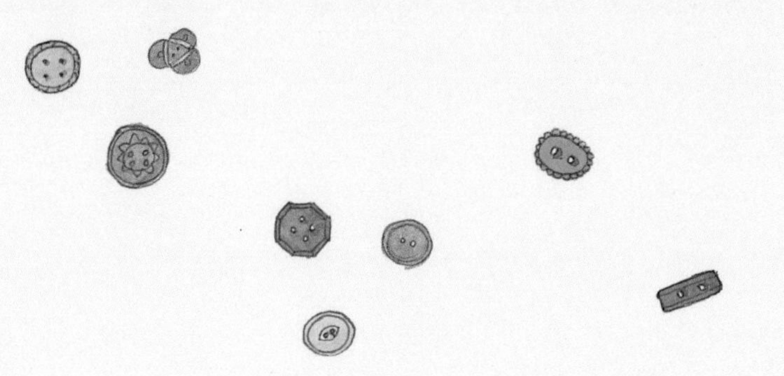

 Published in the United States by Doubleday, an imprint of Random House Children's Books, a division of Penguin Random House LLC, New York. Originally published in Australia by Angus & Robertson, an imprint of HarperCollins Publishers Australia Pty. Limited, Sydney, in 2012.

Visit us on the Web! rhcbooks.com

Educators and librarians, for a variety of teaching tools, visit us at RHTeachersLibrarians.com

Library of Congress Cataloging-in-Publication Data is available upon request.
ISBN 978-0-593-12346-1 (trade) — ISBN 978-0-593-12358-4 (ebook)

Cover and interior design by Natalie Winter
The illustrations in this book were created in pencil and watercolor.

MANUFACTURED IN CHINA
10 9 8 7 6 5 4 3 2 1
First U.S. Edition

For my wonderful parents,
Cynthia and Patrick

Ruby Red Shoes is a white hare.

Ruby Red Shoes was given her name when she
was a baby. Her tiny feet would get as cold
as river pebbles, so her kindly grandmother
knitted her a pair of red shoes.

They were the color of radishes
and when anyone tried to take them
off her feet, she would squeal.

COUNTING CARROTS
1 2 3 4
5 = BUNCH
STARS

Since then, Ruby has always worn red shoes.

Ruby Red Shoes lives with her grandmother
in a prettily painted caravan.

Her grandmother's name
is Babushka Galina Galushka.

"Babushka" means "grandmother,"
"Galina" means "calm,"
and "Galushka" means "dumpling."

She is soft and cuddly
and smells of violets, which are
her favorite flowers.

GG

Babushka Galushka encourages Ruby to be
an *aware* hare, treating everyone's feelings,
as well as her own, with great care.

"Feelings are just like delicate birds' eggs," she likes to say.
"Be as gentle as you can with them."

She also showed Ruby how to talk with all animals, plants, and trees and to respect every living thing's important place on this earth.

The colorful caravan
is warm and cozy, and friends
are always welcome.

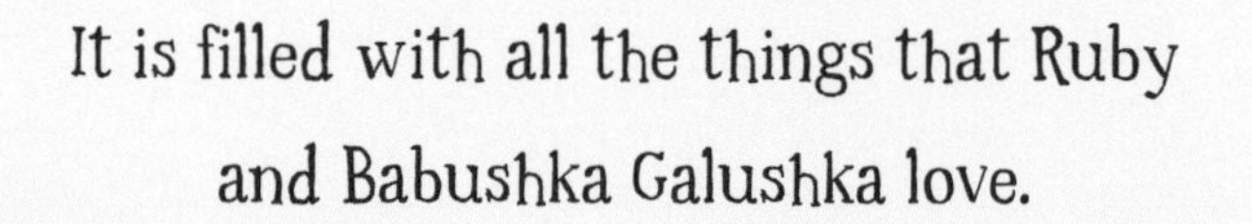

It is filled with all the things that Ruby and Babushka Galushka love.

There are generous teacups for hot drinks,
feathery quilts to snuggle up in,
jars of colorful buttons,
and posies of flowers in pots and jugs.

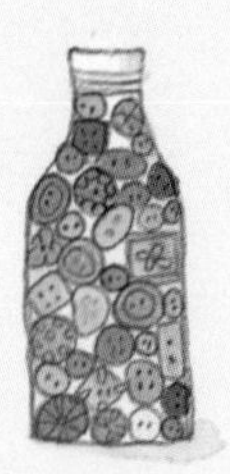

There are soft, warm chairs
and places to drift off and snooze.

HAREY
STORIES

One of Ruby's most cherished places is
the glorious deep bathtub. It sits on
grand feet shaped like a lion's paws.

Sometimes when Ruby is submerged
up to her chin, she imagines the bathtub suddenly
deciding it's tired of standing still and running off
into the forest with her bobbing along inside.

It sounds like an exciting adventure
until she begins to feel seasick!

Ruby loves gardening and
grows all her own vegetables,
fruits, herbs, and flowers.

Much of her day is
spent in the garden.

There are always many things to do—
seedlings to be planted and watered
and busy, buzzy bees to be calmed with gentle words.

She loves to sing sweet songs
to everything that grows.

The garden is filled with delicious food to eat:

Green peas eaten straight
from the pod.

Sweet, happy mint.

Crunchy carrots cut into

twigs for snacking.

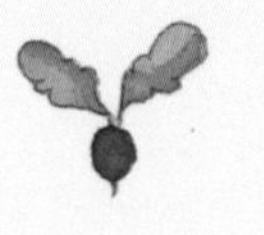

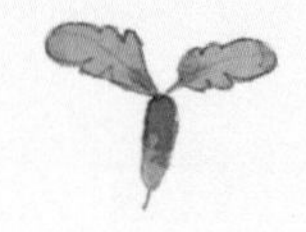

Ravishing radishes.

Blushing peaches.

Blackberries, which make little hands
a pretty berry color.

Ruby's wonderful garden is also home to a jazzy group of chickens.

Ruby gives the chickens all the things they need to be happy—a safe and comfortable home and tasty and nourishing food to nibble.

To keep them fabulously fit, Ruby teaches the hens to play soccer—with plums. They cheat dreadfully!

œuf
=
egg

Ruby's chickens are curious and clever.
They love to learn, so Ruby teaches them
French, which they adore.

Now they ask for baguettes and
croissants to eat instead of
ordinary bread crumbs!

Ruby loves the peace and
stillness in her garden.

The floating butterflies,

dancing green leaves,

and whispering trees are perfect
for soothing an aware hare.

Ruby enjoys little naps in the cool grass.
Often she daydreams, watching the breeze tickling
the leaves or hurrying lazy clouds through
the powder-blue sky.

The clothesline makes happy
snapping noises as the billowy linen
tries to fly away with the wind.

After a busy day in the garden, Ruby
welcomes bedtime, and Babushka
Galushka tucks her under her
cozy quilt and reads her a story.

Together they look out at the marvelous,
velvety night sky and thank the millions
of magical stars staying up all night
to watch over their happy caravan.

Good night and sleep tight.

Natalie McComas

Illustrator and artist Kate Knapp is a graduate of Queensland College of Art, in Australia. Her Ruby Red Shoes books are inspired by her family in England, and Babushka Galushka is based on her English grandmother. Kate lived in London for three years in her twenties, but now lives in Queensland, Australia, where she runs a design studio, Twigseeds, which produces greeting cards, stationery, books, and housewares. *Ruby Red Shoes* is the first book in her Ruby Red Shoes series. Learn more about Kate and Ruby at RubyRedShoes.com.au.

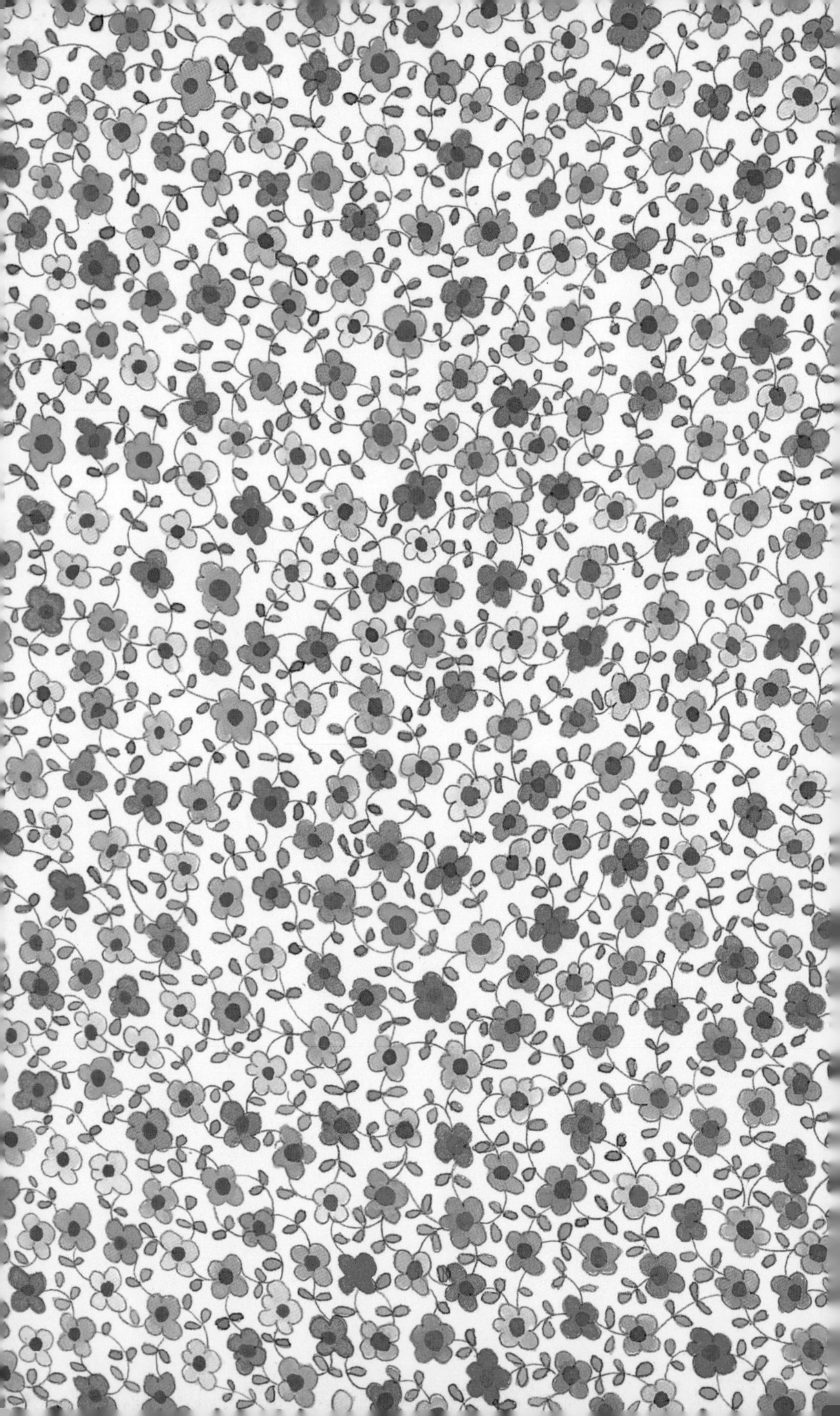